Waterslain

Poetry by the same author

COLLECTIONS

The Rain-Giver
The Dream-House
Time's Oriel

SELECTION

Between My Father and My Son

LIMITED EDITIONS

On Approval
My Son
Alderney: The Nunnery
Norfolk Poems
Petal and Stone

TRANSLATIONS

The Battle of Maldon and Other Old English Poems
Beowulf
The Exeter Book Riddles
The Anglo-Saxon World

EDITOR

Running to Paradise: An Introductory Selection of the Poems of
    W. B. Yeats
Poetry 2 (Arts Council – with Patricia Beer)
The Oxford Book of Travel Verse

Waterslain

and other poems

Kevin Crossley-Holland

Hutchinson

London Melbourne Auckland Johannesburg

Hutchinson & Co. (Publishers) Ltd

An imprint of Century Hutchinson Limited

Brookmount House, 62–65 Chandos Place, London WC2N 4NW

Hutchinson Publishing Group (Australia) Pty Ltd
16–22 Church Street, Hawthorn, Melbourne, Victoria 3122

Hutchinson Group (NZ) Ltd
32–34 View Road, PO Box 40–086, Glenfield, Auckland 10

Hutchinson Group (SA) Pty Ltd
PO Box 337, Bergvlei 2012, South Africa

First published 1986
© Kevin Crossley-Holland 1986

Set in Linotron Bembo by
Input Typesetting Ltd, London SW19 8DR

Printed and bound in Great Britain by
Anchor Brendon Ltd, Tiptree, Essex

ISBN 0 09 164291 4

for Sally, my sister

Contents

Acknowledgements and Note

Poems from the cycle 'Waterslain' were first printed in *Agenda, Ambit, Between the Lines, Country Life, Literary Review, London Magazine, London Review of Books, The Ontario Review, PN Review, Poems for Poetry 84, Poetry Durham, Poetry Wales, The Scotsman* and *Thames Poetry*; and other poems in this book first appeared in *Agenda, Country Life, Encounter, The Ontario Review, Poetry Review, Poetry Wales,* the Schools' Poetry Association's *Footnote* Series and *The Times Literary Supplement.*

Sixteen poems from 'Waterslain' were included in the programme of that name produced by Fraser Steel and first transmitted on Radio 3 on 21 November, 1985. 'Mortar', 'Beachcomber' and 'Warden' have been broadcast on Poetry Now (Radio 3) and 'Beachcomber' on Radio Norfolk.

I am indebted to Peter Dale for his perceptive and detailed comments on a draft of 'Waterslain' and to Sally Festing and Gillian Crossley-Holland for their helpful comments on individual poems.

While writing 'Waterslain', I have returned to *The Story of a Norfolk Farm* by Henry Williamson (Faber, 1942), *Kenzie* by Colin Willock (André Deutsch, 1962), *Fishermen* by Sally Festing (David & Charles, 1977) and *The Shore Shooter* by Alan Savory (The Boydell Press, 1983) which was first published under the title of *Lazy Rivers* (Geoffrey Bles, 1956). I have also looked with renewed interest at the paintings of Matthew Smith. The found poem 'Local Historian' consists of words and phrases taken from the booklet *Saint Clement's Church, Burnham Overy* by Audrey Earle (Cambridge, 1963), and includes part of her quotation from *Nelson* by Carola Oman.

WATERSLAIN

1 Lifeline

Between skywide fields
shadow-ribbed,
crammed with wurzel and beet,

and the salt quarterings'
shine and shift,

this lifelong earthwork stands, squares
its lumpen shoulders,
raised boundary between
mainly earth and mainly water,

Coke, Woodget, Townshend, Nelson –
contrary lives and livelihoods.

Fibrous dark cord
from the hazelnut cluster and
granaries and maltings in desuetude

to the gold ramparts bristling
with marram, shingle ridges,
skirl of the ocean
singing old songs about the Pole.

2 On the Dyke

Years back,
still on the first green leg
a boy walks side by side
with his fair-haired younger sister.

How earnestly they talk!
How little they miss of the world
between us!
They've ambushed almost half the tribe out
in the slant sunlight!

I can hear their voices
far off and very clear . . .
For as long as I watch
they come on towards me.

Laddie first, riddling
mussels on the Hard,
and Fred stepping out with a good-looking dame,

then down to the dark pools tepid
and chill,
Diz dabbing for her supper.

They corner St Vitus,
eager for spoils,
advance on laughing Agnes . . .
pass up luckless Bodge.

At the first elbow
they begin to frisk and shout;
they scramble, somersault,
vault this whole embankment

first breached and sandbagged in the Great Flood,
forgetful once more
under wild rose, silverweed, spurrey.

A wave from the Warden
and they're out on their own again . . .

It's afternoon and slant
and of all places in England
I walk here today,
this lifeline and frontier at Waterslain.

3 *Warden*

There's no way to summarize it.
It is all it is
refracted in the ocean mirror.

I can tell you
a tale about Harra the Denchman there
and a homesick Viking
whose bones lie among the serpentine galleries.
Where will that get you?

Or point you where
in this shine
of sand-dune and shingle-ridge and mud
the bittern nests . . .

But that would be telling!

There's little the moony owl
does not know, old and white-eared,
because it is old,
because it listens, because it watches
under red Betelgeuse
and the slow wink of Algon.

Williamson said:
'Wild geese are the genius of the place.'
No! They are whatever in ourselves
is proud or purposeful
caught up in air,
each part of some skein and solitary.

Listen
and the empty sky
soon rings with overlapping song.

4 Mrs Riches

A screw of peardrops
ready for each milk-white child
arrived late
last night from miles inland.

Through the gloom
in that low-slung stockpiled room
proofed with boxes
her growl conspiratorial:

'Owd Billie's gone.'
'Sin what Vic ploughed up?'
'McCullough's buyin' into Hunst'n.'
'Vitus found a walrus.'

And that once, horrified,
leaning right across her counter:

'Foive at Heacham
and Wilkie's houseboat wedged
up East Harbour Way
and that owd MTB
dumped on the quay at Wells
and sin the sandbags
and first owd Arthur knew was water
through his keyhole . . .'

No tale, not even this,
quite all told
in this spiced corner of paradise,
the bell always being rung.

5 Diz

Easterlies have sandpapered her larynx.

Webbed fingers, webbed feet:
last child of a seal family.

There is a blue flame at her hearth, blue
mussels at her board.
Her bath is the gannet's bath.

Rents one windy room at the top of a ladder.
Reeks of kelp.

'Suffer the little children,' she barks
and the children – all the little ones –
are enchanted.

She has stroked through the indigo of
Dead Man's Pool
and returned with secrets.

They slip their moorings. They
tack towards her glittering eyes.

6 Billy

Every year a new draft,
this buoy replanted, this groyne half-
dismantled, the Cockle Path patched up,
and the Mouth itself narrower, wider . . .
For how, since Ararat,
can earth or sea ever be satisfied?

He knows these creeks inch by inch,
their silt and shining, their dark complexities,
and when to shoulder the *Rosemary* into action,
veterans both of Dunkirk.

'C'mon, then, me bootie!'
Infirm and elderly and eager young
he hands from jetty into bows,
a salt shepherd
gentling doubts, winking at such high hopes.

Eyes pale blue, say lace agate,
as the North Sea never is.
Eyes that on a clear day
see over a thousand scrolls
to the end of the world.

7 *Diddakoi*

The wheel of swart water
noiseless
that whirls above the dead, retracted eye;

and the spiked piers that never
impaled Hitler,
still hungry for landings;

the four cracked sails,
shining whore berries
and on Gun Hill the frayed red flag;

and Joan
with her duff pegs and sunset scarf –
not her light
fingers or wide hips

but the craft,
the blood,
and the patterns on the sands
before the tide absolved them:

in the same black breath
speak them.

8 *Goddess*

for Sally Festing

Out of the flint-grey wave,

skin nacreous, mouth generous,
chrysalis in stockinette
one-piece
hideous!

Or you sail in a tub, head thrown back.

Who eats and sleeps only
as the tide allows
restless in the ramshackle grass-green cage
long since ditched by LNER.

You scoff at the shinglers
with no eyes for sky or sea;
you spurn as childish
pétanque and rounders.

Ocean's apprentice,
learning to move as she moves.
Novice in the parliament of fowls.

Almost an elder sister,
and always.
Untouchable.

9 Bodge

He is their cracked mirror
and the boys don't like what they can see:

the work of a cruel caricaturist –
a boneless dumpling
who grins too long and blubs too much,
upper lip always damp with snot or sweat.

Elbowed out of their secret councils,
their expeditions
cockling, crabbing, cycling the lost lanes,
he teaches them their cruelty.

And on the beach alone
under the sky's awnings,
shy of the sea's claws,
he gives back their sense of loneliness.

Pink and fluttering and maimed:
seldom, they discover, can the tongue sing
just what the heart means.

Quintain debagged;
bloated windsock, crumpling.

Only later do they come on
the Christian virtues.
In the mirror each face suffers a smile.

10 Shuck

From saucer pulks
where pale light lingers longest
we made his eyes.

In this seedbed only think:
Dead Hands wave, Things worm,
marsh lights flicker.

We made his blood from arteries
obsidian in the moonlight,
his hair from shaggy sea-purslane.
His chains are chains of marsh mist.

Skriker, Hooter, Fenrir:
these are his blood-brothers.
We gave him the howl of wind
carried from Siberia.

And witnesses?
With terror or with damp black
earth, one way or another
he stops every mouth.

11 Beachcomber

Faithful as a wordfisher,
there he goes, old magpie of the foreshore!
Face chafed and chapped like driftwood.

Parcelled shapeless against
winds straight off the icecap
but look! agile even so, jumpy as a tick,
quick in his pickings.

Scoofs along the tideline scurf,
his oily sack full of consonants:
hunks of wax,
and seacoal, rubber ballast, cork,
sodden gleanings.

And swinging in that shoe-bag hitched
to his broad belt?
Ah! In there, sunlight and amber moonlight,
emerald and zinc and shell-pink,
Aegir's vowels.

12 Mason

Brylcreem, broad shoulders, goofy smile:
one strayed from the set of cigarette-card heroes
collected on the wide sands
in Cromer and Skeggy.

Half-a-dozen beach-boys and tomboys
cling to his neck,
catcalling, caterwauling
as over the saltings he powers his DUKW.

'Hey! Wanna ride my amphibious daughter?'
Cobb at Bonneville! Campbell at Ullswater!

'OK, see yer later . . .'
Down at the Garage, kids soon into gear
on raspberry vinegar, ginger beer –
spins on the plate of his steam engine
shunted out into nettles . . .

Rock, rock, rock around the clock,
kick against the pricks,
an always-rebel, necessary flambard

defining by opposites –
no less than this sheer light –
all this space
and breathing silence.

13   The Great Painter

Though his spirit
possesses that house as surely as
violet shades course through the creek,
shutters blind the windows from month to month
and salt cancers the royal blue.

He has escaped to sweets
at St Columb, and Paris and Provence,
a plump indulgent wavelength
of pink and crimson, viridian, ultramarine.

The lines here are too Lutheran:
flat-chested dunes,
the ruled horizontals of marsh and ocean.

Too near the bone!
He shuddered when the wind's mouth framed
its forbidding questions.

Not for him
light honed on a northern whetstone,
the burning ice of aurora borealis;
nor was he the first to flinch
at this ruthless incandescence,
too cutting even for Crome and Cotman,
still awaiting a master.

14 Caretaker

When the tarmac's in a sweat
and Poker's field is waterslain,
his leafy books curl up like shrimps.

That serves him right.
The staithe needs life, not furriners,

only
so little life is left:
nothing but dregs up Norton Creek
once ploughed by shingle boats and whelkers,
black silt over landing stages,
a poor crop
of children unlikely to stay.

It's the same with half his class:
no thought except for Number One.
They would've pumped
not sucked
if this place were not a plaything
but their heartbeat.

Old fule!
You can squeeze his bleeding walls.
Dry, I write. *Dry*.

15 Local Historian

a found poem

A low flat coastline, sand and saltmarsh;
and a streak of light,
bright as fish scales . . .

Up to 100 tons, malt, coal, corn and oil-cake;
the great granaries and maltings
all converted . . .

Ceased to be
cruciform. Mutilated; mutilated;
now form the Brothercross
on the little green below the church.
Squat, crouching tightly;
the wind sweeping in from the sea . . .

Paid for destroying of Jackdaws;
Paid Gam Gregory
for spreading the mould in the churchyard;
Payd to Joseph Bobbit for a Book
which is concerned with distemper which now rages
amongst the horned cattle;
Paid for 12 Jackdoyes (jackdoyes 3 a 1d.) . . .

A very gruesome story:
in the year 1307
William Umphrey, chaplain, and Robert de Orleyns
boarded his ship,
bound his hands behind his back until
the blood gushed out at the nails,
imprisoned him until . . .

As a boy Horatio Nelson;
a short cut through the churchyard;
the headstones bear many names still very familiar –

Woodget, Parr, Haines, Scoles, Riches, Thompson,
    Mason . . .
Have gone; remain; in spite of; whirlpools;
think; walk; rustles;
windows.

16 Wildfowler

Seven sounds in the pallor.

The sound of the silent assassin –
a slice of white moon
between his teeth.

The sound of no-wind,
nothing but pressure in the silent frame.

Then sleeping water,
not stertorous or small-sighing,
still lost in some dark sliding dream.

The mutter on the marsh
and at once its antiphon –
Banjo's shallow breathing.

Now it comes,
the thickening of air,
the rush of wings
and passionate sky-voices:
a spring of teal,
then mallard, jinking redshank, widgeon.

The No. 4 out of the Magnum.

Great clump on the marsh, splash in the creek,
and Banjo's off!

– All before the opening
of day's intricate soundbox.

17   Vic

Stirs; quite delicately sips;
yawns over Friday's yellowed *Advertiser* . . .

Outside is cold as inside
is cold, wind flights over the marsh,
the walls of the sky drip
as Vic already rises,
eases himself out, pink and primed,

into the beginning –
shapes still inchoate,
pewter on oyster, seacoal on zinc.
Time never was for pondering.

Banjo far-off on the brew!
A taste of plickplack in the air!
No smell of sharp rain!
His sense of day is animal
and utterly secure.

Crossing the yard,
he gossips
with passerines in the thistle scrub;
hails and cajoles the two Suffolks
(the black gelding and chestnut mare)
into the shafts . . .

Didn't you see his wading walk?
That almost inward smile?
He is this land's stage manager –

dawn corrugator,
trawler of a thousand screaming gulls –

overseer
in the candid light
watching you for one moment
longer
than you watched him.

18 John

Unlike that *shiten shepherde* down the road,
his staff is duty, his smocking
self-effacement,
as if he thinks to keep his head
well down might enable his flock to win
a better view of God.

Time has not incised his face but moulded it.

After the Black Death's lapping,
the sea's recession:
oyster-men and salt-men and samphire-gatherers,
they all followed
the singing tideline,
turned their backs on this flint hulk
(thirty years and still unfinished)
in the lee of the hill.

Not lost in the mind's labyrinth –
unmoved by the sophistry of disputation,
the ecstasy of mystics –
but always on the road, spinning
round his parishes 'held in plurality',
year by year he has sought
to narrow that old gap between
man and God.

His slow smile is part of God's promise.

'Listen,' he says. 'Only listen.'
He listens in prayer,
as vacant as his beaten church
circled by spirits of wind.
He listens to the Word –
King James' tidal cadences
that follow the heart's contours.

There was a man sent from God . . .

19 Miss McQueen

Gong Lane and greengages:
this morning in the orchard
I coached myself and coaxed myself
to walk alone
again:

application gets you so far.

Could've! Should've!
I never realized.
Sometime mistress of parabola and paradox,
almost finished, schooling cabbages.

This one body . . .

And now you bring me
flagrant poppies

and yes I know
John will come with communion later.

Reproofs! Consolations!
When all I see
is splayed legs, still coltish,
eyes bright in their bone stoups,
one last refusal.

20 Laddie

King
of the small pool.

Trooper, tussler, accruer, custodian.

Watchful and terse
as the luminous cat-tide rises
and *Duck* and *Golden* swing
then straighten
on their anchors – his engines
fuelled
on whelks and summer passengers.

The black shingle barges: his.
The mussel lays: his.
Silvermilk slakes won by Several Order.
And when the water drops back
and drains, he tracks trespassers
with huge binoculars.

Horsewhipped at thirteen.
Brought an action against the farmer.

Rowed provisions under fire
across the Tigris.

A salty word; the snick of a smile:
in no way prodigal
but English and not to be crossed.

And now
he is watching,
holding court and watching
as this spring tide still rises,

creeps through the marsh,
floods the capillaries,

until there is such a shining
as far as far Trowland and Scolt Head,
unbroken
to the line of the sallow wave.

21 Tertiary

Down a lane holm-oaks
hallow, all but islanded by drifts
stocky and immaculate –
snowdrop, anemone, marguerite –
Old Agnes flourishes.

Seasoned perennial,
rubicund and rotund, always affable,

she leads pilgrims out
to the green hollow
(earth springy, then giving)
and the silent ferment sweet to the tongue,
the nipples flowing.

'Here is the canal
the poor souls row down to get provisions . . .'
Suffused with lily pads and bulrushes.

'This is the aching arch
of departure and return . . .'
Grey-green with lichen, crumbling.

'And here is their Dormitory . . .'
Stones for pillows.

So very little reason
why they should not be
here, white habits, white cowls,
thronging this place.

22 *Publican at* **The Hero**

Often I wish I had been born
taller. And this nag wishing
is even worse than the lack of inches.

And boss-eyed . . .

I hate them,
phlegm-coughing, ash-tipping, piss-taking,
sour as sloes, hunched over
their exclusive games of euchre and dominoes.

It's 'Emmie this' and 'Emmie that',
winks and sauce and innuendoes.
And Emmie? She would humour them.

Dear, dear Waterslain:
Shit Creek your other name.

What even do they know
of that painted face,
so staunch, so strangely feminine,
whose whole life was this proving?

The things we ought to have done . . .
Fire . . . First man in . . .

Nothing and nothing.

23 Old Lag

Sucked off my soldiers'
green and khaki uniforms, come to that!
Stripped them down to uniform blue-grey.
Must've got into the blood stream!

So here's the story:
Sunday night, late,
cloud cover, wind offshore.
Up top it was perishin'.
I just peeled them off like peachskins,
easy as that.

Unfastened the suspenders
and rolled them down sexy as stockings.
Roped them, lowered them,
SCARPER!

No, and duffed up one
of them ugly leerin' gargoyle-things.
Never could stand them.
Bloody reptile!

A bleedin' waste, all them empty churches.
Give us our daily bread,
that's what I say,
a blessed slice of self-service!
You know the words, old son:
Heaven helps them who help themselves.

24 Furriner

That rumpus on the staithe,
all that flap and hoisting
as the tide rises;
reunions at the Moorings;
coronas of light in the quiet houseboats:

you
may call it artificial,
this summer respiration;
I say the place choked on its own silt.

On the rocks, was it?

Every month another
shell for the wind to moan in . . .

What is unnatural
is this shoal of shiny Midlanders,
traipsing and sinal.
Not ratty, we call them.

Just as it is, was it?

No, when I round the bend
in the scalding lane
and see that immense, almost-empty theatre –
breathing marsh,
signals of the sea –

I say I have reached home.

25 Leaving

On this tall dyke
where I have walked and watched
there was a meeting.

Under the fizzing hard blue light
you must narrow your eyes at,
generations dovetailed
and half the village quickened:

gossip's sharp spindrift first,
then those considerations that seldom
trouble children – dark tides
tugging at every anchorage in the creek.

It grew late . . .

It was my own children
leaped from me,
looking in all directions.

They surge down this lifeline
here and now
towards the gold ramparts
and the skirling sea,

and still, high over them and me
and the sea-acres, the land-acres,
the gulls criss-cross
like stitches, like nets, like arguments,
like love.

COMING HOME

Mortar

Up and down the streets silvered
by winds sharp from the estuary
the dangerous walkers patrol:
causes, cries and short straws
and, for once, we close the door.

Slain god and godlike slayer
lie on the desk, embalmed
and musty; these are
the other times, between the lines
of mythologies and histories:

days of kitchen-scabbards
and the split log's singing,
gleams and stitches in time,
consequential household offices
and the big O of a yawn.

You've been busy with bulbs
today, I with the drill,
both with tack and nail;
out at the back I burned
cuttings while you cooked:

it is a part-song punctuated
by unspoken recognitions;
not until day ended
did we pause, smile, begin:
'It's at times like this . . .'

And kiss. So we proceed
by indirection and, observing
the rituals of this house,
its ordinary maintenance, mean
one thing: the pointing of mortar.

Greening

What happens, this efflorescence,
Is more like lace, then more like foam,
Than leaves. You wake and, early-morning
Myopic, peer through the half-stewed
Window, and there, on the swaying bush
You have seen flourish in New England,
There is a stitching of unmistakable green,
Pointed as work from Nottingham or Honiton,
The delicate articulation of spring.

You unbolt the back door and a film
Of rust, fine as talcum, falls to the cracked
Linoleum. This is a magic threshold,
The concrete traversed by an early-to-work
Snail whose opal trail shimmers in the sunlight.
So early still and the walled garden
Is already hushed, its plate of night rain
A magnifying glass. Grow, shoot, bud, swell:
What is it but a young girl sounding
New words until she has possessed them?

'Now the green blade riseth . . .' and this heart
Quickeneth at the all-at-once profusion
Of signs and songs: the birds' anticipation
That woke you this morning at ten-past-five,
The honeysuckle so quick to redress
Its short back and sides, the moss
Vulva-plump over the course of the drain,
Crocus already limp, stunned by sunlight . . .
And out into sunlight you wheel your autumn
Daughter, and set her, crowing, under stripling oak,
Its foam an impossible paean, Badedas-green.

Birds and Fishes

In a dustbin
piteously piping;
on a raft of paint shavings
and sodden petals,
her dark eye gauzed,
your sister the fledgling.

Still arching
and swimming through air
among hopping sandflies
on a lumpen grey spur,
still unready,
your sister the minnow.

Cradle and cotton wool,
all the care we can muster:
and it is true –
alleluia! –
you are pink and lithe and merry.
But that history

of silences, small sicknesses,
sudden falls . . .
At midnight you cheep.
We hurry to your door
and find you on your nose, sleeping,
arms stretched, palms up.

Preparatory School

Licker Lonsdale could tap dance.
His hot eyes stripped us
naked so Murdoch the Mole used to burrow
beneath his blankets before
lights out.

Unlike Henry's generous backhanders
(purple stripes on the badge of the buttocks),
Grummet's half-nelsons brought me to my knees.

Holland had some pox and was nicknamed
Morbus.
He left the term before I came;
thus I was accorded his name.

Hymn 25 in the *Public School Hymnbook*.
The day thou gavest, Lord,
the one day between now and half-term.
My tears lolloped on to the page.

Coronation Week, Sunday sweet shop,
lashing Henry's horrible daughter
to the crumbling Wellingtonia . . .

And up the usual decrepit drive,
past mature trees
and the scoreboard showing the whole team
out for 13.

I listen to the silence of your preparation
for the mad dash
past the vulturine crucifix
into the gloom,

then angrily reason with myself
all the way from Otford west into Dorset
watching your reflection
in the mirror
dissolve.

Happy Birthday

for Dominic at 16

How do you do, bone-house?
Here's another stepping-stone
on this risky journey –
another pause for understandings:

three pawns are worth more
than a bishop; the more I give,
the more I have to give;
no perspective without humour;

panache wins admirers; to act,
always to be my own audience;
language ties and language cuts,
mightier than Excalibur.

You will bother to read this
and take issue with it
one way or another
almost as a matter of principle.

You have a sort of spiky grace,
like a conker in its armour,
a crocketed spire, the elbows
and knees of the contrary sea.

Happy birthday, bone-house!
Here's another stepping-stone
on this risky journey –
another pause for understandings:

remember the child I'm leaving;
work against small wars;
today colours tomorrow; I will
not miss the boat to the stars.

Woman Sorting Redcurrants

Her back is still straight but
her eyes are bleeding.
Through the honeysuckle trellis
where she sits and sorts
swarm the domestic atrocities.

Again and again she tells
their names and their names
do not control them . . .

This sweetness is almost
unendurable. With her pale
wrist she dabs at her eyes;
unheard, the perfect drops
patter into the kitchen chalice.

The Guardian Tree

Unlike that manor oak
in Northamptonshire
it did not climb within our walls,
right-angle with the roofbeam,
and overhead explode
into a flurry of leaves.

Out in Iceland
on the howling farmsteads
solitary trees graze outer walls,
they lean against each other
in mutual dependence.
It was not like these.

No dragon gnawing at its root,
no eagle in its high uneasy branches,
no deer, no goats
tearing at the green shoots:
nothing fabulous or universal.
No fructifer, no seductive
sweet dew on its leaves,
no spirit-ladder.

We seldom gave it thought:
a guess at its age
and surprise it survived a bomb
meant for the Docks;
a second desultory guess
(being neither children nor trigonometrists)
at its huge reaching height;
though we fretted at its red scab, and peered
for the lost canary,
and raked and cursed and
carted off its leaves,
and once, one June evening,
we made love beneath it,
inviolate

as its green arms
waved away the world.

Not only bereft now;
abandoned, as children by a mother.
It was our cap of happiness,
rough-tongued and embracing,
our pennyplain guardian tree,
rooted in earth but
free of doubt and cause and argument,
rising above change.

Orkney Girls

1 Girls at Skara Brae

The place is a hiss.
                    The cells
and passages and womb-houses, runes
of sandstone under their turf skin,
all of them defused, bleached
into static.
                    Turn your back
on the usual slop and clout
and the summer blandishments
winking in the meadow.
                            Then enter,
listen . . .
                    In the white wave
are the hiccups and polyps
and such subtle modulations
the heart decodes.
                        Nothing singular,
but in this sunken room
amongst dresser, hearth and cot,
shafted by sunlight, repossessed
after five thousand winters,
this persistent broken
singing:
            Spring and a necklace . . .
scattered seed . . . now and here
and now . . . all our ripening.

2 The Girl at Gurness

I become little more than a voice:
a bruck of bones earth-fingered,
all unravelled and unlimbed
by salts and seep and vapours.

There! The whale-path to a farm
on a fiord, a girl in sunlight;
that road to the Irishman, clover
on his tongue, and the whirlpool of love,
and that is the way of the dove
to Jorsala. I have no knowledge
of where that way leads my brothers
with blooming axe and scramasax.

I am only in shadow saying,
Look at the rib of water passing –
the show of aquamarine, limpid,
and the lumpen everyday swell,
the furious spears of black-and-silver;
saying, Look at the shift of light
gilding the bare breasts of Rousay.

The wind is a wearisome impartial
scold. Think of the ways you also
took, or did not take . . .

(Mouth stopped. Two shoulder brooches.
An iron knife. Also lobster-shell,
an unbroken necklace, blushing pink-and-lilac.)

3   *Stromness Girl*

Her father's fathers came in
from the north, brewing and salty,
the women from the south and west –
violet Caithness, the concealments of Antrim,
locking the flint-grey ring.

Red ribbon in her hair, parts her lips . . .

Her subject is the smash and glimmer,
that sweep of the scythe intent
on shearing. After which there is
poor rest, no terra firma, risky footing.

Eyes lace agate. Painted shell necklace . . .

Oyster and pearl, not one wrinkle:
she tells of seeming and dissimulation,
elaborate surface tension above
the röst blood-dark and churning.

Glib. All glitter. Flashy rings . . .

Does not walk so much as slide
and swing. Wholly abandoned
to her legend, she shrieks with laughter,
collapses, sobs on any shoulder.

I am what you want only . . .

Gags first on a skuther of gutturals,
softens, sideways drifts in a mirror
of assonance. How her old story still
enthrals us. Shape-shifter
at the whirlpool that grinds men to dust.

Dying, with Birdsong

St Titus Basilica, Gortyn

The old man sniffs, drowses.

Birds strike up in the basilica.
Matutinal section of sparrows
catapult through apertures
in the crumbling chancel,
perch on ledges, airily.
The apse is sharp with grace notes.

The old man stirs; they disperse.

He opens bread, masticates,
sniffs, drowses. And back they
come, a headful, rangers
of the vanished nave, jinking
between olives, bearers
of desiccated wild grapes.

Talley Abbey

Is this the symmetry of God?
Which is not cool,
and moves and does not move,
depleted not incomplete.

Dark block, rough block;
one minatory yew.
And, through which I think
I see the wrestle and blue

surge of such contours,
stone on serious stone:
devotion's arch upraised
and still like hands at prayer.

Angels at St Mary's

'The angels have gone.'
  Church Guide, Walsham-le-Willows

Up among bleached stars and suns
Are the tongues, protruding, oak pegs
Wanting their smiling high-fliers.

The fledglings heard black hints
And saw battle-lights advancing.
They conferred, they spread their wings.

Or did they become spirits of
Themselves? Angels rearranged,
Acute angles where clear sound and

Sunlight cross? They are in the air.

The Word-Mantle

Those ladies at their looms! What
is to become of us?
                I wear
this traveller's mantle
and they will not catch up with me
in the souks of Bodrum
or the amazing wheatfields
or head sky-high
amongst the lapis domes in Samarkand.
I will outfleet them.

I wear time's mantle
and they will not reach me beyond
the midnight crossing.
Let the border guards arrest them and
turn them into pumpkins!
Or else:
I will leap the great ravine
into the arms of the New Year
and leave them behind ravening and
powerless.

No?
I have this third mantle
and as they seize
another dancer
by the hair on the back of his head,
and cut the thread,
it will rise and stand in my shape –
beyond their shears and skills
this honest word-shadow,
still singing.

Behind

I leave behind the toad, a study
in warty brown concentration
hunched over the drop. I leave
the aloof air, its pale sleeves
of cirrhus, and the pink-tipped
corn. I leave the cutting
edge that is never duplicitous.

Light-headed, weightless as saints
after this long levitation:
the port wing dips, the starboard,
I am a cloud-slalomer, inspector
of siren crevasses; rising
still rising, the strict compounds
that schooled me singing in my ears.

A Walsham Harvest

The sky: violet and then
and only then
in this right-angled honest place
so intense it quivered.
It broke the rules.

Fire's glottals
hacked through hedge and thicket,
its pale scarves trussed
the bullace the lichenous crab apple;
crack cracked the willow.

So the moon loped
up, quickened
in the breathing spaces,
over the blond corn
this lopped thing, this ladle of blood.

Foggy and very close, one blast
to begin
this evening of long intervals.
Cough; creak; creak; scuffle.
All ears and stoops.

On the Way East

The terminus smells of wild garlic,
The buttoned cloth is squirrel red-brown.
There are depths as black as black holes
Where the barley has been beaten down.

The caparisoned elms are alight
(Each stilled in a flood of gold fire).
Such dawdles! Standstills! The white
Skyline is lanced by a crocketed spire.

Wild roses cling to pink brick. The track
Is burning sienna. Almost, almost free!
Beyond the hectares of mangel and beet
Open silver-grey arms, stunning, the sea.

Comfort

Who said anything about comfort?
Those syllables do not rhyme
with zinc slakes or ice-bright sky.
The sea is grinding her spears.
Up creeks and gullies, over groynes
the black tide surges
and the hag wind rides her.
In the bleak forest on the staithe
rigging clacks and chitters.

Little but memory for company,
wild geese, swans whooping,
but no urbanity no
gossip prejudice bitterness sham.
In London I dream of these harsh folds,
the sea's slam, the light's eagle eye,
and here again I draw
this place – hair shirt, dear cloak –
around such infirmities.

Eastern Light

for Jonathan Crossley-Holland

There was a time
when so little seemed uncertain.
I lounged beneath the green seigneurs
and viewed the huge sky stooping:
rinsed, I wrote, and *ringing*,
and *fluent*, and *lapidary*.

The light was a bright statement,
candid and clean as a Commandment,
a sword-stroke
admitting no half-measure.
Doubt itself seemed a sin.

In this indeterminate and empty
quarter, this mesh
of sanding and marsh and creek,
I see this is creation light;
unblinking light, severe and immense.
Does that mean it is true?

That boy climbing the dune's escarpment,
scrambling to the top of far Gun Hill
comes so close
we could call out to him.

In this frame
almost innocent of dampness
and bruises and concealment,
the tricks-in-trade of the misty west,
is there one blade,
one fault, one silver serpent,
you think you cannot clearly see?

You see what you think then?
Where is the deceit in equity?

Look east. Light of light.
I go back to the beginning.
Apparent, I write.

Outsider

No return, there is no
way to return
except the way of the exile
to an area of absence.

Poor frayed sack, tired bone-sack,
slumped on the form in a sea of dock.

Look! Where the dark tide infiltrated
the Plate from four quarters
and covered the coiling casts,
there are dunes knotted by marram.

And the dizzy mill is shorn of her sails.
Squats glum and black
listening to the warm susurrus in the barley.

He supposes he still loves the place,
not for better for worse,
only for echoes booming
within him as the rare bittern booms
on a deserted shore:

stumps of crab apple and quince,
the green shine on the jetty's rotting stanchions,
and Sanskrit in the mud, and still
that same tang of iodine when the tide's out.

Matrix, he says, old matrix,
so much changed, so much missing,
so little he has not already remembered
in his creation.